Λ
R
R
I
O
R
S

DATE DUE

		SEP 2 1 2002	
		SEP 0 9 2002	

)riau

Talonbooks   •   Vancouver   •   1990

published with the assistance of The Canada Council

Talonbooks
201 / 1019 East Cordova
Vancouver
British Columbia   V6A 1M8
Canada

Typeset in Baskerville by Pièce de Résistance Ltée and printed and bound in Canada by Hignell Printing Ltd.

First Printing: October 1990

Rights to produce *Warriors*, in whole or in part, in any medium by any group, amateur or professional, are retained by the author, and interested persons are requested to apply to his agent, Des Landes, Dickinson et associés, 4171 Hampton Avenue, Montréal (Québec), Canada H4A 2L1, who is authorized to negotiate.

First published as *Les Guerriers* by VLB éditeur, Montréal, Québec.

Canadian Cataloguing in Publication Data

Garneau, Michel 1939 -
[Guerriers. English]
Warriors

A play.
Translation of: Les guerriers
ISBN 0-88922-282-7

I. Title.   II. Title: Guerriers. English.
PS8563.A66G8313 1990   C842'.54   C90-091575-7
PQ3919.2.G37G8313 1990

Les Guerriers was first produced at L'Atelier du Centre national des Arts, Ottawa, Ontario, on April 6, 1989, with the following cast:

Gilles   Robert Lalonde
Paul   Eudore Belzile

Directed by Guy Beausoleil
Designed by Guy Beausoleil, assisted by Louise Lemieux
Assistant Director and Stage Manager: Roxanne Henry
Photography and projections: Jean-Claude Labrecque
Sound track: François Myrand

This first production was co-produced by Théâtre d'Aujourd'hui and Théâtre français du Centre national des Arts.

A second production by Fondation du Théâtre Public was first performed at Festival international des Francophonies in Limoges, France, on October 11, 1989.

Warriors was first performed in English at the Martha Cohen Theatre in Calgary, Alberta, on January 25, 1990, with the following cast:

Gilles   Brian Torpe
Paul   Peter Smith

Directed by Glynis Leyshon
Sound by Allan Rae
Set and props design by Terry Gunvordahl
Costume by John Pennoyer
Lighting by Steve Isom
Fight Director: Jean-Pierre Fournier

The play was produced by the Alberta Theatre Projects, playRites '90, and presented in association with Victoria's Belfry Theatre.

THE SET

a set
on which or from which
images
cosmogonies
views of the earth seen from the moon
can be projected or can emerge
not essentially images of combat
but also texts
treaties
ads
drawings and photographs of military fashion

the function of this iconography should be clear:
the context of the show is
ostensively
history

armchairs   sofas
an exercise machine
a tanning couch
a microwave oven
a small freezer-fridge
television sets
vcr machines
cd players
computers

these appliances could be sculptures
evocative images at least

the costumes are luxury sportswear

although the characters drink a lot
they are never drunk   sometimes tipsy
hyper-stimulated by coke   coke reigns

paul smokes cigars
gilles steals a few puffs occasionally
but he is often tempted to smoke

the pauses indicated are real pauses:
four or five real seconds long
the silences are longer than the pauses

Peace brings affluence,
affluence brings pride,
pride, anger,
anger, war,
war brings poverty,
poverty, humanism,
humanism, peace,
which brings affluence
and so goes the world.

Luigi Da Porto
(16th century)

Warriors, to speak about war
and especially about the military industry,
as we experience them here:
inside; as an idea;
as an economic reality;
as a cultural reality.

I was born in 1939 and my first memories
are of 1945.
The children born in those years are
the children of warriors.
(Often funny warriors,
most of whom didn't know what they were defending
or what they were attacking but they had been convinced
of a duty that needed their youth.)

Mass culture states very clearly
that the dominant value is money
and that the ultimate pleasure, the ultimate solution
and the ultimate honour is violence.

When preparing *Warriors*, it became horribly obvious
that we do not think,
and have never really thought about the phenomenon of war,
and that it is, therefore, still feasible
and the majority of the inhabitants of the planet earth,
whether devastated or indifferent,
believe that war is possible, probable, inevitable, imminent.

War has so many impotent accomplices: all of us . . .
We are the *Warriors*,
We-ourselves, we-others, we-all.

Michel Garneau, 1989

WARRIORS

Day One

gilles is sleeping in his armchair
he is obviously dreaming
it is obviously a nightmare

he curls up fetally
lets out a scream
the scream we let out
when we dream we are dying

screaming wakes him up
mad

GILLES:
    chrrist i'm sick of dying like that!
    (an exorcism)
    aaaaaaaahhhhhhh!

he tries to fall asleep again
then sits up and waits
stiff and uncomfortable

pain in his left side

11

aw no!

it's a little stitch,
short but violent

he massages his left arm
then whistles
eine kleine nachtmusik
calms down
starts to fall asleep again

the door slides open silently
in walks paul
looking jovially mysterious
he is carrying several bags
including two from the liquor commission
puts them down   grabs   before even
taking off his coat   it's winter
one of the liquor commission bags
takes a bag out of this bag
then the box
he opens the box and takes out
the famous velvet bag
and out of the famous velvet bag
comes the bottle

PAUL:
      chivas regal royal salute

he opens the bottle
sniffs   hoots
lets gilles sniff
appreciatively in a lyrical groan
paul after more howling
and groaning pours
reverently
and they toast
cautiously
sip bellow toast again
sip again   roar

12

GILLES: *(softly)*
   shii

PAUL:
   fuu

GILLES:
   chrr

they drink   their eyes closed
little sips
the glasses are emptied   refilled

PAUL:
   mercy
   mercy it's so good

they savour

GILLES:
   not bad

little sips for a long time
till all is calm   extremely slow
then paul still looking mysterious
unplugs the phone
gilles looks at him   inquisitively
paul walks out with the phone
and comes back without it

GILLES:
   ah

PAUL:
   uh huh

GILLES:
   right

paul   still slowly
opens his briefcase and takes out
a file which he waves in the air

PAUL:

   my dear partner
   you went out and got us the contract
   for the cigarette that is milder
   because it's slimmer
   and i dear partner
   i think i can safely say
   that i went out and got us
   the contract of a lifetime

GILLES: *(woefully)*
   aacch don't tell me it worked

         he curls himself around his glass

   the army contract

         he tosses back his drink and extends his glass
         paul fills it for him

   national defense
         (a long moan)
   ohhhhhhhhhh

         pause

PAUL:

   if i hadn't figured out
   that it's precisely because

   you've got a beautiful soul
   inside a tormented conscience
   under a great cloak of morality
   and   a crown of ethics

14

that you are the best idea man in canada
you'd really piss me off
but i figured it out

GILLES:
about time

PAUL:
now i understand
i know that you suffer
i know that everything makes you suffer

pause

you even stopped smoking

· *paul finishes off his drink*
pours another   takes out a cigar
lights it   gilles watches
the cigar
paul offers him one
gilles refuses   painfully

so suffer but think
that's all i'm asking
think my friend think
besides i know i can tell
you've already started

gilles empties his glass slowly

GILLES:
great stuff really great

PAUL:
great and expensive

they savour

15

do you think it's expensive because it's good
or that it's good because it's expensive
like some fools claim

they drink

best scotch in the world

if i had opened a bottle of royal salute
and discovered that it was rot gut
i could have objectively decided that there is a kind of social
justice which leads the wealthy to pay through the nose
for rot gut but objectively i opened
a bottle of royal salute and it was
the legendary pure-velvet cat's pyjamas
my daddy always talked about
so there's no justice

GILLES:
there's poetic justice
but you can't always count on it
it's a real reality with an element of chance

they drink
paul nurses his cigar
with relish

PAUL:
whaddya mean?

GILLES:
eh?

PAUL:
what's the link between reality and chance?

GILLES:
some people seem to think
that realities can exist
where there is no element of chance

16

PAUL:
oh

GILLES:
and those people usually have no sense of humour
not in the real sense i mean

PAUL:
no real sense of humour

GILLES:
right

PAUL:
which doesn't exclude chance

GILLES:
or tragedy

PAUL:
right right

        paul stares at his cigar

GILLES:
so we got it

PAUL:
yessir

        gilles sighs
        paul refills the glasses
        and sits down in his armchair

GILLES:
they accepted our bid?

PAUL:
uh huh

GILLES:
    crazy bastards

PAUL:
    rich bastards
    they're rich
    very rich
    the richest

        long silence
        so everyone can think about
        the money in national defense

    yeah
    but
    (solemnly)
    there's no life like it
    that's what
    we gotta beat
    you understand that's precisely what
    they want us to beat
    there's no life like it
    go further than that
    do better than that
    more

GILLES:
    there's no life like it

PAUL: *(in dumb admiration)*
    there's   no   life   like   it

            silence

GILLES:
    the first time i saw it
    i thought they're outta their skulls
    soldier means war means death
    no no means life
    no death there
    you don't go into the army to die

you don't go to war to die
you go to war to kill
like life

PAUL:
it's brilliant
everyone saw it
everyone went wha wait
what are they saying?

that the army means adventure risk
risking your life is the height of living
like car racing
a brush with death is really living
courting death means living twice as hard
three times
the army means adventure all expenses paid
yeah

GILLES:
denial simple as that
just denial
not bad as a basic idea
deny the obvious
just say no

the first thing that comes to mind
is wrong
you think the army is a ticket to death
think again
c'mon try a bit of imagination
it's a ticket to life
simply   let it be said
and it shall be
a ticket to life a career ticket
a ticket to fun and games
and the toys are beautiful
jet fighters
supersonic bombers
electronic spy planes
tanks that cost as much as a small town

19

nuclear submarines where whole towns of men live
giant helicopters

> *pause*

PAUL:
    guns knives uniforms

> *pause*
> *a gesture from gilles*
> *paul passes him his cigar*
> *gilles takes a puff*
> *and gives it back*

GILLES:
    have you ever tried to imagine how it would be
    to die in a tank   imagine   a tank on fire

PAUL:
    well

GILLES:
    eh

PAUL:
    c'mon   that's   i mean that's
    nowhere to start   if   really
    i mean
    if people started   imagining   if people

> *silence*

    there's no life like it
    you have to start with that
    then forget it
    it's all in the slogan

    everything else is designed to fit the slogan

    you know that

GILLES:
  no kidding

PAUL:
  but you ha haf hafta start with
  just thinking about it gives me palpitations

GILLES:
  it's the scotch

PAUL:
  no no
  i don't think so
  it's kinda like
  stagefright
  i guess
  i dunno if i can say that
  i'm not an artist
  it's like being scared
  and excited at the same time

  because this time we gotta
  gotta be crazier than ever
  we're gonna hafta trust
  totally trust our craziness
  gonna hafta trust

GILLES:
  ridicule

PAUL:
  well

GILLES:
  totally trust ridicule

          silence
          paul isn't sure
          what's happening
          he starts to say something
          decides not to

uneasiness
paul puts out his cigar
they drink
paul searches through the bags
gilles closes his eyes

PAUL:
i found some books

GILLES:
how are we gonna operate?

       paul takes some books out of a bag

aren't we gonna bring in the whole gang?

PAUL:
have a seat

GILLES: *(his eyes still closed)*
this is as seated as i can get

PAUL:
i got the contract because i promised
i mean it's in the contract
that we're gonna deliver the goods
i mean an outline of the campaign
the basic idea
and especially the slogan
a week from now

       gilles his eyes still closed
       moans

now don't panic

       paul waves a book in the air

we've got lots of documentation   lots of research material
you usually like that

GILLES:
  yeah

PAUL:
  so

GILLES: *(very sarcastic)*
  what would i do without you

PAUL:
  ha ha

        he shows him a book

  on war

        gilles opens his eyes

  by carl von

GILLES:
  clausewitz

PAUL:
  you heard of him

GILLES:
  yes

PAUL:
  a german?

GILLES:
  yes

PAUL:
  great we can't go wrong
  i mean when it comes to war
  they're the best

GILLES: *(closes his eyes again)*
        just try not to be such a racist

PAUL: *(proud of his sense of humour he lays it on)*
        you can't be a racist about germans
        you can be racist about negroes
        about chinamen arabs indians
        most of all you can be racist about the damn jews
        but not about germans no way
        it's really convenient

GILLES:
        clausewitz

        aiee aiee!

                his eyes wide open
                he clutches at his chest
                on the left side
                he massages his chest

PAUL:
        what's wrong with you?

GILLES:
        i must've eaten something
        i've got like a stitch
        like little shooting pains
        on the left side
        i dunno maybe it's my

        do the intestines come up this far?

PAUL:
        you wanna go home?

GILLES:
        you putting me on

PAUL:
    not really
    but if you're gonna get sick
    tell me right away

        pause

GILLES:
    right

        silence
        they look at each other

    clausewitz
    always wanted to read that
    it's a classic
    but i can't say i really feel like it
    right now

        paul gives him the book
        gilles looks at the book

GILLES:
    now available in penguin paperback
    shiitt

PAUL:
    what?

GILLES:
    forget it
    too hard to explain

        more looks
        gilles scornful

PAUL:
    i hate it when you do that

        pause

GILLES:
i know

> *passive hostility from paul*
> *gilles is reading clausewitz*
> *paul looks at him reading*
> *then he takes out another book*

PAUL:
treatise on polemology

> *gilles stands up*

gaston bou bou bouthoul professor at the institute
of social studies   vice-president of the international
institute of sociology

> *gilles takes the book*

GILLES:
the sociology of war

> *he starts reading while walking*
> *back and forth slowly*
> *massaging his left arm*

PAUL:
by the same bozo bouthoul   in pantheon books we have
the girl at the bookstore was real nice
ugly but nice   war   and that one essay on
polemology   it was funny i mean i say i'm looking
for books on war   she says what war?
are you looking for any particular war?

> *paul takes two tv dinners*
> *out of the freezer and puts them*
> *in the microwave oven*

i said no   war   she said thirty-nine forty-five?
i say no   war   she says well come see
eighteen i dunno what or nineteen-fourteen

nineteen-thirty-nine korea algeria vietnam weapons
aircraft battleships a whole section this long
chock full i say no i think he's gonna want war in general
she says who's he?

he takes a bottle of wine
out of a cupboard and opens it

chateau margaux!
she says oh well that's funny   on war   period
i don't know what we've got   no one ever
asked for that before
mostly people want art books
on guns battleships airplanes
that's what people usually buy
look   along those lines   i bought this one

he shows gilles a luxury edition
on arms and armour
gilles glances at it

i bought it for myself
it's a nice book
lots of pictures

gilles is still pacing
back and forth reading

so we finally found bozo bouthoul
and this one   glucksman   the language of war
and   the height of power   um   that's what i
found to get you started   all things
that you're interested in
had you ever heard of
pology?

GILLES:
    polemology
    no

PAUL:

you're interested in it though
should be stimulating for you
usually when we come across new material
you really take off

GILLES:

are you assuming that i'm gonna take this on?

PAUL:

no no i'm not assuming anything
i'm just trying to see if

a long silence they look at each other
it should be obvious that gilles is
about to leave

PAUL:

no but   well   listen   for years now
you've been talking about   taking a year off

GILLES:

right

PAUL:

ok   here's the deal   you get through this week
you find us a great slogan
then   you take your sabbatical year that's right
full salary   a whole year   to the day

a long pause

GILLES:

two

silence
looks

PAUL:

you can't take advantage of the situation like that

GILLES:
  oh yes i can

  silence

PAUL:
  you bastard

GILLES:
  eh?

PAUL:
  lousy sonofabitch

GILLES:
  hey   watch it

PAUL:
  two years

GILLES:
  two years
  full salary
  two years
  to the day

  paul writhes around like a man
  trying to break loose   mumbles
  grumbles
  sighs

PAUL: *(a sad murmur)*
  oh
  alright
  you win

GILLES:
  put it in writing

PAUL:
  don't you trust me?

GILLES:
  i've read our partnership agreement

  pause

PAUL:
  you're just trying to make me feel good

GILLES:
  does it make you feel good?

PAUL:
  yes

  pause

GILLES:
  is it true we've only got a week or

PAUL:
  we've got exactly ten days
  and that's the truth

  gilles looks him in the eye

  it's true
  i swear

GILLES:
  put it in writing
  all of it

PAUL:
  ok ok

GILLES:
  right away
  spell it out
  we've got ten days
  i've got two years sabbatical
  full salary

in a row!
two consecutive years
beginning ten days from today

>*paul is writing on the word processor*
>*gilles watches him*
>*two copies are printed out*
>*gilles reads his*
>*carefully*
>*has paul sign it*
>*signs it himself*
>*paul puts his copy in a drawer*
>*gilles puts his in his pocket*
>
>*silence*
>
>*they look at each other*
>
>*paul pours some scotch*
>*they drink*

GILLES:
we got everything we need?

PAUL:
everything

GILLES:
you in good shape

PAUL:
A1

GILLES:
i'm not

PAUL:
i know

GILLES:
but you don't know   how bad

31

PAUL:
    i can tell you're about to tell me

    he waits

    sooner or later

GILLES:
    it might be a bitch this time

PAUL:
    i'm ready
    i got the best shit in town
    if not in all of north america
    want some?

GILLES:
    no
    not yet

            paul prepares one helluva line
            of coke and sniffs it mystically
            then sits down at the word processor
            and starts typing away

PAUL:
    i'm opening a file

            he types and chuckles
            gilles reads
            the microwave oven announces
            that the tv dinners are ready
            paul takes them out
            they eat and drink the
            chateau margaux (that is paul
            has a bite to eat and drinks the wine)
            while listening to the news
            on american pay tv

            BLACKOUT   IMAGE   BLACKOUT

Day Two

GILLES: *(reading)*
       "war is an act of force
       and there is no logical limit to the application
       of that force
       each side compels its opponent to follow suit
       a reciprocal action is started
       which in theory must lead
       to extremes
       to disarm the enemy is the aim
       of any act of war"

              paul takes his clothes off
              puts on some tanning oil

PAUL:
       act of war   i like it   act
       action act
       always hafta put sex into
       everything
       violence   light
       weird i just associated violence
       with light

legal patriotic glorious violence
that must be where the light comes from
it's like oil glistening on muscles
glory
always hafta make it a bit wild
animal freedom
if you can get just a flicker
in the back of the mind a good old flash
of rape murder
anonymous murder
nothing personal
anonymous and sexy
always hafta remember the slumbering attila

GILLES:
spare us the grade school lessons

PAUL: *(settles down on the tanning couch)*
i'm just trying to help

GILLES:
i don't need your help!
what i need

        a shooting pain

        aiee aiee christ almighty fucking hell

                —   *he stands up walks around*
                    massages his arm
                    waits
                    does some cautious exercises

PAUL:
uh

GILLES:
never mind

PAUL:
  sure
  sure

GILLES: *(picks up his reading again)*
  "if you want to beat your enemy
  you must match your effort against
  his power of resistance
  which can be expressed as the product of two
  inseparable factors
  the total means at his disposal
  and the strength of his will"

PAUL: *(from the tanning couch)*
  you can't eliminate the allusion
  to sex
  look even in there's no life like it
  there was the allusion to
  the good life   eh
  and what is the good life?
  it's

GILLES:
  would you mind keeping
  your obsessions to yourself

        paul looks at gilles
        who goes on reading

  "the frequent truces in the act of war remove war
  still further from the realm of the absolute
  and make it increasingly a matter
  of assessing probabilities"

        paul extracts himself from the tanning couch
        and pours them some scotch

PAUL:
      yeah yeah yeah

GILLES:
 "therefore only the element of chance
 is needed to make war a gamble
 and that element is never absent"

PAUL:
 what?

GILLES:
 what what?

PAUL:
 what's never absent?

GILLES:
 chance

PAUL:
 ah

> *they drink*
> *cocaine all around*
> *the complete ceremony*
> *then gilles picks up*
> *his book again*

GILLES:
 "not only its objective but
 also its subjective nature makes
 war a gamble"

PAUL:
 who is that?

GILLES:
 clausewitz

PAUL:
>
> i like it   great stuff clausevitch
> associating violence and gambling
> as long as you don't leave out the sex
> it's bound to work

GILLES:
>
> yeah right the sumerians were into that

PAUL:
>
> what do the sumerians

GILLES:
>
> back in the epic of gilgamesh
> violence games sex are all intimately related

PAUL:
>
> right but

GILLES:
>
> don't worry
> we'll come up with something
> absolutely disgusting

PAUL:
>
> i ask for no more

GILLES:
>
> by trusting my talent   for ridicule

> *paul is thinking*

PAUL:
>
> what do you mean by that?
> i don't really follow you
> just what do you mean by ridicule?

> *paul puts his clothes back on*

GILLES:
>
> when i first started out in this field

PAUL:
not the old story about your boss's wife again

GILLES:
i already told you about that?

PAUL:
there's not much you haven't told me

GILLES:
hmmm

pause

there were i don't know how many of us

PAUL:
where?

GILLES:
holdfield and crown

PAUL:
oh right

GILLES:
there were seven eight of us
we were looking for a slogan
for the egg marketing board
we'd tried everything

PAUL:
the deep think tank

GILLES:
you better believe it
and i was the youngest of the bunch
i didn't say much

PAUL:
those were the good old days

GILLES:
> very funny
> your sense of humour is always so fresh
> invigorating
> and most of all so original

PAUL:
> you gonna tell your story
> or not!

> > *pause*
> > *gilles takes a big sip*
> > *of royal salute*

GILLES:
> i was watching them all   trying to learn
> a week had gone by with ten consenting
> adults coming out with the stupidest things
> the craziest most
> far-fetched ideas   the dumbest jokes   the feeblest
> plays on words   enough to drive a moron crazy
> fourteen hours a day

PAUL:
> yeah

GILLES:
> we were babbling idiots   i couldn't believe it
> full of lousy coffee   stomachs shot to hell
> wrecked   with thousands of words
> that just kept trotting around
> in your mind

> > *paul is really enjoying this*

> your mouth   your whole body
> we were exhausted   fed up   at our wit's end
> pathetic

PAUL:
> hey it must've been great

GILLES:
> so i decided the job really wasn't
> for me   that i clearly couldn't take it anymore

PAUL:
> attaboy   you sure haven't changed

GILLES:
> i despised them   the whole pathetic
> bunch of bananas
> i decided i was gonna leave right then and there

PAUL:
> what else is new

GILLES:
> they were all ranting and raving
> i stand up
> i start to leave
> i open the door
> and suddenly
> i get such a lame-brained such a
> pitiful   such a dumb asinine ridiculous idea
> that i figure
> i've got nothing left to lose
> i can't sink any lower
> i may as well finish off this shitty mess
> in the thick of the shit
> may as well tell them   so i turn around and look at them
> there's so much smoke you'd think
> the whole lot of them had gone up in flames
> i open my mouth and out it comes   like vomit
> get crackin'

> *gilles is out of breath*

PAUL:
> so you're the one!
> you're the genius who came up with that!
> too fucking much! you never told me that!

GILLES:
    i walk out and slam the door
    in the hall i can hear them yelling
    shouting with joy

PAUL:
    no wonder

GILLES:
    clapping
    someone comes running out and grabs me
    spins me around
    kisses me hugs me
    it's a standing ovation
    my boss is religiously writing on the board

        paul says it along with gilles

    get crackin'
    they're all delirious   some of them are crying
    and i start laughing in spite of myself
    laughing and crying at the same time
    then out come the bottles
    we start to have a few drinks
    partytime   the deed is done
    and i'm the one who did it

        gilles is really out of breath

    get crackin'
    that's what we were looking for
    all week fourteen hours a day
    they put me on the permanent payroll
    gave me a raise
    a new office
    for the most half-assed thing

PAUL:
    the simplest

41

GILLES:
　　the most idiotic

PAUL:
　　the most effective

GILLES:
　　the most moronic

PAUL:
　　you either laugh or you groan
　　but you remember it!

GILLES:
　　the dumbest idea i could come up with
　　by resorting to pure and simple
　　unadulterated
　　ridicule

PAUL:
　　it's the results that count!

GILLES:
　　and that's how the great hoax began
　　that's how i became
　　what you call the best idea man in canada
　　and that's why with every new contract
　　i'm always afraid i'll lose my gift
　　for ridicule
　　because it's
　　my creativity

PAUL:
　　at least you've got creativity!!!

　　　　gilles catches his breath
　　　　with some difficulty
　　　　paul looks at him and smiles

42

PAUL:
> wow!!!
> get crackin'
> they kept that slogan for years

GILLES:
> years and years and years

> *paul refills their glasses*

PAUL:
> to ridicule!

> *they drink*

> *gilles is trying hard*
> *looking for ridicule*

GILLES:
> to national defense
> to the army!
> to life!

PAUL:
> to life!!!

GILLES: *(shouting)*
> to death!!!
> *viva la muerte*!!!!
> royal salute!!!!!!!!

BLACKOUT   IMAGE   BLACKOUT

Day Three

PAUL:
> drip drip drip on your head
> subtle chinese method

GILLES:
> hanged by the neck   the feet   the thumbs

PAUL:
> crucifixion

GILLES:
> decapitation   the guillotine

PAUL:
> the axe

GILLES:
> fire   the stake   torching   flame-throwers
> napalm

PAUL:
> electrocution

GILLES:
electrodes on the breasts   the penis   the tongue

paul gets caught up in the game
of seeking and finding

PAUL:
strangulation

GILLES:
the garrote   the firing squad
lethal injection

PAUL:
a bullet in the head

GILLES:
in the neck   the bayonet   the razor blade
dragged by the hair
by horses   by jeep

PAUL:
crushed to death

GILLES:
scalded   molten lead in the inner ear
plunged in hot oil
riddled with arrows
thrown to the lions

paul begins to lose interest
because he's not as quick
as gilles
gilles is fascinated

PAUL:
drawn and quartered

GILLES:
the wheel   the rack   dismembered   seared   scalped
flagellation   nerve gas

radiation   germ warfare
chemistry

PAUL: *(resigned)*
    walled in
    stoned to death

GILLES:
    trampled to death   defenestration
    sensory deprivation
    starvation
    thirst
    drowning
    buried alive up to the neck
    at high noon

PAUL: *(suddenly delighted with his contribution)*
    impaled

GILLES:
    red-hot poker up the rectum
    bled to death   throat slit
    smothered   perforated
    the Iron Maiden

PAUL:
    who what?

        gilles doesn't even hear him

GILLES:
    boiled alive   thrown off a cliff
    gorged
    that's just from memory
    we've forgotten a few   for sure
    we could probably
    go on for hours
    with only what we know by heart
    so to speak
    in argentina in modern times
    the military leaders threw people

46

out of planes into the ocean
austerity measures
if we do some research
just to go beyond our immediate memory
as citizens of the planet earth
we'll

PAUL:
what

GILLES:
humanity
humanity is really marvellous
such imagination
such inventiveness
splinters under the fingernails
the bamboo cage
flaying
it's incredible

PAUL:
just what are you doing?

GILLES:
my god we almost forgot the concentration camps
the gas chambers
the execution of children in front of their parents
the execution of parents in front of their children
the execution of children by their parents
and all the experiments
blankets with tuberculosis smallpox
genocide
all the genocides
the

PAUL:
what are you getting at?

GILLES:
  what?
  i'm thinking   reflecting   searching
  i'm contemplating the subject
  studying the question

PAUL:
  well   let's just say
  it doesn't seem like a very
  positive approach
  to me

GILLES:
  and what do you know?
  what do you know about positive approaches?

  he feels a sharp pain

  awww shhhittt

PAUL:
  c'mon   there is something wrong with you

GILLES:
  pour me a scotch

  paul takes a long look at him

PAUL:
  what's wrong with you?

  *gilles is searching through a
  liquor commission bag
  takes a bag out of the bag
  etc.   royal salute
  he fills two glasses
  gives one to paul who
  sits down sips and sulks
  gilles empties his glass standing
  his balance seems precarious
  he waits   long   tense pause*

48

GILLES:

    i'm fine

PAUL:

    you're not sick?

GILLES:

    just wasted

PAUL:

    yeah well this is no time
    to get sick

GILLES:

    i know dear partner i know
    and i stand here before you delighted
    dear partner to see you in such good health

PAUL:

    just tell me
    if you need
    something

GILLES:

    i've got everything i need

BLACKOUT   IMAGE   BLACKOUT

Day Four

paul is sitting at the computer
running down
a list of words
and clichés
which use
military terms

PAUL:
oh yeah
a big Mac attack

gilles is reading a book

obviously
the vanguard

GILLES:
hey that's interesting

PAUL:
wage a war against violence
to arm oneself

to get up in arms
rank and file
pass muster
a volley of insults

GILLES:
beautiful

PAUL:
but what do you intend to do with it?

GILLES:
with what?

PAUL:
your military vocabulary

GILLES:
if you don't like it
scrap it

PAUL:
but you just said it was beautiful

GILLES:
no i said what i just read
is beautiful

PAUL:
ah

GILLES: (reading)
"we saw admirable things
in the streets in the city squares
we saw mountains of heads
hands feet
the men and the knights were
stepping over corpses strewn everywhere
on the steps and inside the temple
we rode our horses

in blood up to the rider's knees
up to the horse's bridle

just and admirable judgement of god
who wanted this very place to receive the blood
of those whose blasphemy had for so long
soiled it
celestial spectacle

in the church and throughout the city
people were giving thanks to the eternal''

PAUL:
what's that?

GILLES:
raymond d'agiles   canon of the cathedral in puy
on the taking of jerusalem

PAUL:
i see
now would you mind telling me
why you're reading that to me

GILLES:
i found it in one of the books
you brought me
you don't like it?
you don't find it
interesting?
another lovely little moment
in the history of humanity

PAUL:
if you ask me
you're on the wrong track

GILLES: *(exceptionally aggressive)*
i suppose you can show me the right track!

PAUL:
yes i can
i know you

GILLES:
you know me!
you know everything about me!

PAUL:
right
and i know when you're working flat out
and I know when you're just fucking around

GILLES:
so
you know all that?

PAUL:
we've been working together
long enough
for you to know that it's
just to help you focus
direct your energy

GILLES:
sure
you can even explain that to me
it's too fucking beautiful
you keep watch over my energy
like a sacred flame
so tell me what to do
i beg you
on bended knees up to the ears
in the blood of the church
i beg of you

PAUL:
lay off

GILLES:
show me the path

PAUL:
> i don't like you trying to humiliate me

GILLES:
> my dear fellow traveller

PAUL:
> i hate it when you try to humiliate me

GILLES:
> show me the way

PAUL:
> lay off

GILLES:
> tao! TAO! TAO!
> oh superior man

PAUL:
> i said lay off!

> *he goes to slap him*

GILLES: *(gently sarcastic and insulting)*
> you're not going to slap me   you miserable
> i'm not some girl

> > *paul yells and lunges at him*
> > *they're two little boys fighting*
> > *gilles manages to slap and hit*
> > *paul*
> > *who throws a tantrum*
> > *screaming   stamping*
> > *punching*
> > *(not too vigourously*
> > *whining little humiliated cries*
> > *that sound a bit forced)*
> > *gilles pushes him away*
> > *and paul lets himself fall to the ground*

> > *IMAGE   BLACKOUT   IMAGE*

Day Five

gilles is standing
suddenly twists with pain
paul is playing backgammon
on the computer and doesn't notice

PAUL:
    sorry 'bout yesterday

GILLES:
    sure sure

paul is playing
gilles is recovering
he feels his chest arm
he walks back and forth
looks drained
as if he can't manage to
concentrate on anything

PAUL:
    it's just that
    i've never been able to get used to

the way you work
the lucidity
the pain

pause

the painful lucidity

pause
gilles grunts

the guilt
total
absolute
weight of the world
the whole world
the descent into the deepest
subtleties of   of

GILLES:
the absurd

PAUL:
right
and your famous talent for ridicule
that's a new one on me
enthusiastic despair
is that it?

GILLES:
close

PAUL:
right to the bottom of the pile of shit
where you find the flower of your creativity

fuck

backgammon
gilles laughs discreetly
paul looks up at him

GILLES: *(softly)*
    you fool

PAUL:
    ah
    stop calling me names

GILLES:
    you fool what did you just say

PAUL:
    what?
    what did i just say?
    i dunno

        backgammon

GILLES:
        you just said clearly
        for the first time i think
        that you understand
        how i operate
        you understand very well
        really
        fool
        you've spent so much time so many years
        playing the fool
        that you've started to believe it
        you're no longer aware
        of your own machiavellian
        stainless steel intelligence

            paul exits from the backgammon

PAUL:
        what are you talking about?

GILLES:
        don't you think i know that
        the best way for you to manipulate me
        is to make me believe that i'm

57

manipulating you
and that you're not very smart
just kinda crooked
incredibly venal
born that way
and that without me you would have ended up
a waiter

PAUL:
hee hee

GILLES:
i know you understand exactly
how i operate
and that everything you do
and everything you say
is calculated to nurture me
put me on the right track

PAUL: *(sylvester caught stalking tweety bird)*
well

GILLES:
i'm your artist
your intellectual
the heart
and you're my politician
my financier
the head

PAUL:
that's one way of looking at it

GILLES:
we're the two forces that make
the world go round
but you're the one who controls the dynamics
you're the leader
i'm the one who works for you

PAUL:
  no no
  it's a collaboration

GILLES:
  sure
  my art my knowledge
  my intelligence
  my generosity all exist
  to serve your purposes

PAUL:
  you really believe

GILLES:
  so that you can achieve your ends

PAUL:
  you really believe i think of all that

GILLES:
  no
  no   it's true
  no
  not consciously anyway

  the funniest thing is that
  i'm the only one
  who can tell you
  what you're doing

  i tell you what you're doing
  but you tell me what to do

  my dear financier
  i have the ability to tell you
  what you feel
  but you can tell me
  what to feel
  that's your revenge
  your first revenge

because the second
the second and last
your most exquisite revenge
is that
once i've produced what you need
you stop listening to me

you congratulate me warmly
and you stop listening to me

silence
looks

PAUL: *(casually   without insisting)*
          yeah   yeah   that's the bond between us
          it's a natural relationship
          between two people
          a fundamental relationship:
          need

          gilles grimaces

          i need you
          you need me
          ours is a fundamental relationship
          our relationship is a collaboration
          our collaboration is a friendship
          our friendship is love

          silence

GILLES:
          oh christ

          he massages his left arm

PAUL:
          listen if you're sick say so

          silence

60

GILLES:
  fuck off go eat shit

  silence
  gilles takes refuge in his armchair
  paul gets on the
  exercise machine
  and goes at it energetically

PAUL:
  when i was little
  i used to wonder
  are we supposed to eat
  our own shit?
  or just any old shit
  we come across?

  BLACKOUT   IMAGE   BLACKOUT

61

Day Six

they're wrestling
it's a game
a reconciliation
they stop
they rest

PAUL:
  the state you're in maybe we shouldn't

GILLES:
  what state
  i'm not in any state

PAUL:
  ok ok

  they rest some more

GILLES:
    right
    so   so
    that means that
    war

PAUL: *(with bated breath)*
    yeah?

GILLES:
    nuclear war
    do you think   boom

              he pours himself a scotch

PAUL:
    how should i know?

GILLES:
    seems to me we can't
    get kids to join the army without

PAUL: *(excited)*
    kids? what kids?

              cocaine
              the complete ceremony

GILLES:
    we can't get kids to join the army
    without making nuclear war seem attractive

PAUL: *(very excited)*
    are you telling me we're aiming at kids?

GILLES:
    obviously
    have to let an idea grow
    a kid has to start
    dreaming of the army young

you can't grab him just like that
at eighteen you hafta get him at ten

PAUL:

you're exaggerating

GILLES:

haven't we always known how to make warriors
out of kids?
hasn't it always been the kid who
goes off to war?

PAUL:

actually it's young people not kids

GILLES:

for god's sake we're all kids till we're thirty
you're old enough to know that
kids are the ones that can be filled with fanaticism
and pride because kids can be made to believe
generously passionately that hate absolutely blind hate
is a noble sentiment an ideal to strive for
because in order to fight you have to believe
you have to be a real believer
you have to believe in the unbelievable
have faith
believe in the absurd the impossible
the absolutely unverifiable

PAUL: *(very interested)*
you make war sound like a religion

GILLES:

that's right! you got it!
all wars are holy wars
there are no armies without religion
without the fatal flaw of faith
kids have to believe
that mysteries become accessible
through the blindness of faith
the most illuminating blindness of all

kids have to believe
in the victory
in the truth
in the purity of their race
the exclusive truth of their religion
the absolute and abstract victory of their country
their nation their race
which are all things that exist for real

PAUL:
    good
    there must be a way of saying that
    in one five-word sentence

GILLES:
    christ!   will you shut up!   you're bothering me!
    wait a minute wait a minute
    you made me lose my train of thought
    pain in the ass
    MY train of thought
    you asshole
    they also have to believe
    believe
    the child warrior has to believe
    in the mystery of the economy
    believe in it totally blindly
    he has to believe religiously
    that the sacrament of the economy
    must be defended   in its holy
    status quo
    that anything which threatens
    the sacrosanct ecomony
    must be annihilated
    by destruction   murder   rape if necessary
    by torture if need be
    it must be defended first and foremost
    by winning
    by loving violence more than oneself
    with all one's blood   all one's sex
    loving to death
    loving death

a brief pause
suspense
paul is waiting

PAUL:

> forget the dark side
> work on the bright side
> faith generosity race
> self-sacrifice
> that's always a good one self-sacrifice

> *scotch and cocaine*

GILLES:

> yeah
> but when he falls off his high horse
> of ideals
> and heroism
> and becomes just another victim
> i'm afraid
> that all the child warrior has left
> is fear pain
> his aching body

> *silence*
> *paul is looking*
> *for something to say*

PAUL:

> sure   sure   there are losers
> but war   war is exciting
> when you win   and that's what we gotta sell
> victory victories the victory over self
> love of discipline adventure and education
> plus the fact that we're not at war

GILLES:

> you sure about that?

PAUL:

> yes

GILLES:
>we could be
>at the drop of a hat

PAUL:
>yeah so they say

GILLES:
>if you want to get the kids
>you can't talk to them about war
>you talk about peace
>ok war is exciting if we win
>peace has to be protected
>and if you can get an education at the same time
>learn a trade
>but that brings us back to square one
>there's no life like it
>no i think we have to
>talk about war but
>in a certain way
>ok enough of this
>the more i talk
>the less i say

>>*silence*
>>*paul watches him*
>>*gilles paces back and forth*
>>*several times*
>>*he's about to say something*
>>*thinks better of it*
>>*paul waits patiently*
>>*then takes out a magazine*
>>*and leafs through it*
>>*goes to the bathroom*
>>*returns*
>>*gilles goes to the bathroom*
>>*paul turns on the television*
>>*gilles returns*
>>*paul turns off the television*
>>*tries to look like he's not waiting*

67

GILLES:
> war is exciting when we win
> who's we?

PAUL:
> us

GILLES:
> only us

PAUL:
> no
> us i guess it means the americans
> them means the russians
> us is us and the americans
> but well we follow them

GILLES:
> some country

PAUL:
> and if we win
> the war's over
> no more russians

GILLES:
> if there was a partial nuclear war
> with an american victory
> would that be moral?

PAUL:
> of course
> at least that's what everyone thinks
> even if they don't admit it

GILLES:
> so immoral would be
> suicidal total
> war
> killing half the world is moral
> killing off the whole lot is immoral

PAUL:
and not very good for business
no more customers
i think that's what everyone figures
when you get right down to it   sentimentality aside

GILLES:
remember god's death?

PAUL:
vaguely
god is dead
nietzsche
nietzsche is dead
god
i read that in some toilet

GILLES:
yeah i mean at some point
everyone figured
if god is dead anything goes

PAUL:
right

GILLES:
the probable destruction of the planet
that's even better than the death of god

PAUL:
yeah

GILLES:
seems to me any sensible person
is gonna try to become i dunno
at least a real crook

PAUL:
yeah you better believe it

GILLES:
no hope no morals
all the gods are dead

pause

our work has already become
empty cowardly dirty dishonest
alienated
but as if that's not enough

PAUL: *(sharply)*
don't think about us think about the kids

GILLES:
let me work
(he shouts)
let me work!

PAUL:
oops excuse me

pause

GILLES:
so nuclear war

> *he speaks very deliberately*
> *he is discovering what he's been trying*
> *to say for a long time*

nuclear war nuclear war nuclear war
i can't do anything to prevent it
and i don't even know if i want to prevent it
because i think deep down inside the ordinary guy i am
the guy who thinks like everyone else
i think that people   will simply be getting what they deserve
and that makes me want to be
a real criminal
if everyone's becoming a war criminal
why not
so here i am assassinating the hope of humanity

PAUL:
    what the hell are you onto now?

GILLES:
    just by doing the work we do!
    using language the way we use it!
    it's assassinating language   emptying it
    filling language with emptiness
    with empty words
    people don't know what they're saying any more
    children sing commercials
    the same artificial values prevail
    in professional politics
    in professional sport
    in professional religion love
    professional love
    so that means that i the twenty-year-old child
    i share some kind of responsibility
    with everyone else
    some kind of anonymous responsibility
    i'd like to be personally responsible

PAUL:
    ah   maybe you're onto something there

GILLES:
    evil   i the twenty-year-old child
    i would like to be personally evil
    a demon
    i would like to feel my wings turn black
    and wake up one morning a real devil

PAUL:
    hmmmm

GILLES:
    and i'd like to kill
    kill personally
    legitimately
    just to tell humanity exactly what i think of it
    just to tell god what i think of him

or her
just to be the greatest
the most desperate
in the face of the horrors to come
just to be ready
just to be able to laugh
when the good guys
push the button for the apocalypse
just to laugh as hard as i can
like a kid in a frenzy of rage
just to come in my pants
like lucifer getting off in a flurry of feathers
just to sing out yes to death
like the apotheosis of a big flashy show
just to devour the cancer   savour it
because   you piss me off right down to my soul
by sharing this meaningless shit with me
with that goddamn intelligent little smirk on your face

PAUL: *(while gilles continues)*
aw fucking hell and goddamn shit
here we go again

GILLES:
because we made a million this year
with beer that tastes like parakeet piss   .
because our wives are sleeping together
they're so bored
because we're nothing but lousy
leather and mercedes fetishists
because we haven't had an honest talk
since we were eleven years old

PAUL:
ok   ok stop acting like a baby

GILLES:
when i was little
i wanted to live a real life
i wanted to make myself understood by animals

so that one fine morning a fox
would say hello to me

silence
paul paces back and forth
pours two glasses of scotch
they drink
paul sits down

PAUL:

you get pissed off
you complain
you talk to me about despair
poor bastard you
don't even know what it is

gilles is surprised
this is a new tone for paul
completely

i
feel no anger no rage
no movement nothing stirs
i can play squash without moving
without feeling a thing
some times when i go too fast in my car
i feel a tiny shiver
a tiny urge to kill myself
i understand feelings
but i don't feel them
and i don't miss feeling them
not really
only thing left from time to time
is the urge for a picce of ass
but that's mostly a bit of leftover pride
you know steal some girl you don't even desire
from some poor sucker
i still enjoy royal salute
the cool crispness of coke
waste
and once in a while

there's one oyster that tastes real fine
like a memory
it's always like a memory
the memory of what i used to feel
before when i used to feel
like an echo
every day i do what every day
brings
like the stuff we do together
no surprises no enthusiasm
no disgust   and no hope
just indifference
indifference
funny word eh
indifference indifference indifference

GILLES:
   stop

> *paul lights up a cigar*
> *passes it to gilles*
> *who takes a puff*

PAUL:
   indifference
   your precious language only exists
   so we can manage to say that there's
   nothing to be said

> *paul opens a can of fancy*
> *nuts*
> *takes a handful*
> *passes the can to gilles*
> *who takes one nut*

life is an escalator
you just hafta be patient
it's automatic
the apocalypse is simply gonna be
like turning off the tv
the apocalypse

i think that life is so absurd
i'm probably gonna be the one
to survive on top of the garbage heap
cause i'm the one who doesn't care

GILLES:
job

PAUL:
job complained a lot

GILLES:
he alternated between complaining
and singing alleluia

PAUL:
well if i do anything
on top of the garbage heap it's more apt to be
sing some kinda hallelujah   right
a quiet celebration
an indifferent so much for that

    silence

GILLES:
why don't you commit suicide?

    pause

PAUL:
too cute
people who commit suicide are saying
look how cute i am i'm gonna die
and my death is important
it's not true it's not important at all

how 'bout you?

GILLES:
me?

he thinks about it
eats a nut takes a sip
asks for a puff
takes it

i'm afraid we'll end up
in some great wisdom
where we suddenly understand everything
i can't be sure
there's nothing after this
what if there's something
like a great wisdom a great light
a great liberation a great intelligence

PAUL:
yeah
that would be pretty terrible

BLACKOUT   IMAGE   BLACKOUT

Day Seven

they stand facing each other
looking at each other
paul is tense
gilles limp with fatique
coffee is brewing in the coffeemaker
and it is ready
paul prepares two cups
they drink their coffee standing
but without looking at each other

PAUL:
   well

      coffee

GILLES:
   yeah

      coffee

PAUL:
   it's

GILLES:
poof

coffee

PAUL:
we're getting nowhere

GILLES:
nowhere
we're getting nowhere fast
we're going around in circles
we're chasing our tail
everything's all clogged up
the army war national defense
children in uniform
it's making me more and more anxious
period

PAUL:
everything makes you anxious

pause

GILLES:
maybe but this time it's for real

PAUL:
oh no what's the difference between
false anxiety and real anxiety
eh
c'mon just tell me what's wrong with you!

GILLES:
forget it

PAUL:
you make faces you grab your left arm
eh the left side the heart side the attack side
so is that for real?
or is it just to get me worked up

to give me a hard time
eh what's going on

GILLES:
i dunno
i've got like stitches
shooting pains
burning sensations

exasperated paul searches frantically
and finally finds a brown paper bag
which he passes to gilles

PAUL:
breathe into that

GILLES:
whaddya mean?

PAUL:
just take the bag and breathe

gilles breathes into the bag
and likes it

GILLES:
hey

PAUL:
you see you're getting all worked up for nothing

breath

GILLES:
amazing

PAUL:
it's not that serious

GILLES: *(he's not listening)*
too much

PAUL:
> things have been worse

> *breath*

GILLES: *(concentrating on the phenomenon)*
> look at that

PAUL:
> go ahead take a really deep breath

> *breath*

GILLES:
> well fuck a duck

PAUL:
> we've got a bunch of
> well leads
> lots of ideas
> some good ideas

GILLES:
> this is really weird

PAUL:
> makes you feel better eh
> anxiety   anguish
> hyperventilation

> *breath*

GILLES:
> yeah phew

PAUL:
> not getting enough whatchamacallit gas
> or whatever
> you just breathe into the bag and

> *breath*

presto you're no sicker than i am

gilles takes a breath

GILLES:
yeah
no more no less?

PAUL:
whatever you say

gilles takes a breath

BLACKOUT   IMAGE   BLACKOUT

Day Eight

they do nothing
for quite a while

PAUL:
two days left

GILLES:
eh?

PAUL:
two days left

GILLES:
we've been holed up here for eight days
today's the eighth day?

PAUL:
right
the eighth day
and we've come up with fuck all

GILLES:

    i'm working my ass off
    i swear it's true
    i'm wracking my brains
    i'm trying for real
    the world has become too complicated
    there's nothing you can say
    in a single sentence
    you can no longer say
    live free or die

PAUL:

    oh yeah why?

GILLES:

    what does that mean today?
    freedom?

PAUL:

    don't ask me i never knew
    what people meant
    by that word

GILLES:

    you'd hafta say
    free enterprise or die
    or socialism or die
    or
    we're in the yellow pages!
    we   are   in   the   yellow   pages!
    WE   ARE   IN   THE   YELLOW   PAGES!

PAUL:

    who you talking about?

GILLES:

    the army national defense war
    you can't play on any other feelings
    no other emotion except the seriousness of business!!
    listen
    we're the army

we're a big
important company
something serious
profitable
therefore
we are in the yellow pages!

PAUL:

no it's not catchy enough
i don't feel it

GILLES:

listen listen

the canadian armed forces
we're in the yellow pages

we're just another business
but a big business
there's no business like it
we're in the yellow pages
no risk no violence
no death no pain
there's no business like business
the show is war
war
doesn't matter
it's business that counts
you don't understand
the army for yuppies
the army for reasonable young people
the army for the well-behaved child
right it's good

PAUL:

sorry but it doesn't get to me
i don't like it

GILLES:

they're milder because they're slimmer
you didn't like that one either!

84

aren't you ever gonna understand how it works
the only thing that matters is the magic words
right now
words that are already magic
we can't make them magic ourselves
people make them magic
all we can do is identify them
then use them
mild slim that's magic
but this one's even better
business that's totally magic!
but we're saying it subliminally!
it's completely irreproachably low-key
it's cool detached reasonable
we're in the yellow pages

PAUL:
    it's not catchy enough not snappy enough

GILLES:
    snappy is out these days   stupid
    catchy is out
    cool is in
    reason is in
    plain dumb reason no discussion reason
    reason that is right
    so right it doesn't need to get mad
    at the unreasonable
    security is what counts these days
    common sense
    young people are getting married for money!
    with no guilt
    with reason on their side   righteousness!
    these days a young person can join the canadian armed forces
    because it makes good business sense

    we're in the yellow pages

        very long silence
        paul goes through a series
        of physical antics

85

paces
makes faces and grimaces
gilles repeats his slogan
several times

PAUL:
uh uh nnnno
nothing doing
i don't like it

GILLES:
christ you're dumb
thick as shit
stupid idiotic imbecile
half-wit cretin retard zero

PAUL:
yeah maybe   but you know
i'm a good test
a really good barometer
if i don't like it
the average young person isn't gonna like it

GILLES:
how can you say that?
how can you tell me that?
to my face
how can you be so convinced?
you've always been wrong!

PAUL:
yeah but this time i know young people
average young people
i go out!
i know what they like
and i know they're not gonna like that

and besides you know what our agreement is

GILLES:
i know what our agreement is

PAUL:
    sorry

GILLES:
    still

    no listen free your mind
    imagine beautiful images
    superbly high tech
    imagine the beautiful voice saying
    the reassuring voice
    reassuring but still young
    saying

    the canadian armed forces:
    we're in the yellow pages

            gilles waits

PAUL:
    no
    no
    definitely no

            silence

GILLES:
    i am absolutely convinced
    that you are totally wrong
    once again

            he lies on the floor face down

PAUL:
    maybe
    but we can't take any chances
    not with a contract like this
    two days left

GILLES:
one day left
just one day
i've had it for today   fini   kaput

long pause

PAUL:
ok
wanta watch a movie?

gilles thinks about it

GILLES:
guess so

paul puts a cassette into the vcr
they watch the beginning
of a porn scene

GILLES:
what the hell is this?

PAUL:
a skin flick

GILLES:
you crazy?

paul stops the cassette
takes out another

PAUL: *(resigned)*
ok ok
i asked them to choose a classic for you

GILLES:
what

PAUL: *(reading)*
    "the battleship po tem kin"

      gilles groans
      painfully

        IMAGE   BLACKOUT   IMAGE

Day Nine

gilles breathes into his bag

GILLES:
 i bought a dog

PAUL:
 wha
 when?

GILLES:
 just before we began
 he wasn't two months old yet
 so i couldn't bring him home right away

 otherwise

 as soon as we get outta here
 i'm gonna go pick him up

> *breathes into the bag*
> *as a joke he offers the bag to paul*
> *who accepts it laughing and takes a breath*

and laughs and takes another breath and laughs
and passes the bag back to gilles
who breathes into it from time to
time

PAUL:
what kind?

GILLES:
chowchow

PAUL:
the kind that looks like a lion
sortof

GILLES:
sortof

PAUL:
why that kind?

GILLES:
because konrad lorenz said
it's the most catlike of all dogs

PAUL:
whatshisname lorenz a vet?

GILLES:
yeah

PAUL:
so your dog
what does he look like?

GILLES:
he looks faithful
i'm gonna call him sesame
you know the most difficult thing
to figure out in a dog
is his way of thinking

no two dogs think alike
hafta figure out how he thinks

PAUL:

and how do you figure out
how a dog thinks

GILLES:

you begin by deciding
you're big enough to raise a dog
take him on as a disciple
in consciousness
you hafta be ready to let the dog sense you
right down to the deepest instincts
and you hafta get him to accept
being sensed and directed

pause

PAUL:

i was in love with a newfoundland
once
when i was twenty-two

pause

he drooled a quart of saliva an hour

long silence

did you know
that my father died in the war
when i was a baby?

GILLES:

no
i didn't know that

PAUL:

yeah
my father died in the war

when i was
a few months old

pause

GILLES:
a hero i suppose

PAUL:
right   a real hero
he blew himself up with his own grenade

gilles laughs snorts
paul too
laughter peters out
sadly
silence

GILLES:
well my father
died one whole summer long
in the hospital

but towards the end of the war
he rivetted pieces of tanks
or maybe it was destroyers i dunno
he was real proud of that

i mean
once he told me
that he was real proud to have done at least
that
for the war
one of the few things my father ever told me

my father had trouble talking
physical trouble
wasn't used to it
never learned how
he grunted
i never heard him say yes or no

93

i always heard him grunt
something that sounded halfway
between the two

in the hospital he kept saying
it's not fair it's not fair
he thought that dying wasn't fair
my father really missed the boat
about death

PAUL:
are you working now?

GILLES:
no
i'm not working
i'm not working anymore

PAUL:
ah

pause

GILLES:
but you're still working

PAUL:
yes

GILLES:
you can't stop yourself

PAUL:
no

GILLES:
well i've decided i'm gonna learn how to stop

*gilles takes a deep breath
in his bag*

the whole family was gathered round the bed
the heat was a real kil . . .
and that hospital smell   the roses
my father was half dead half asleep
suddenly he opened his eyes   real wide

he takes a breath

he looked like a surprised little kid
we all drew closer
because he looked like he wanted to say something
he did say something   he said

goddam i feel like taking a shit
he fell back onto his pillow
let out a long wheezing breath
we just stood there without moving
my mother stretched out her hand slowly
shaking
the whole family was shaking
my mother closed his eyes
and then we all burst out laughing

they laugh
a bit

sometimes i think
that was one of the most profound things
ever uttered by a human being
just before dying
sometimes

very long silence
gilles feels like crying
and doesn't want to
he swallows and swallows
paul pretends
nothing is happening

i can't go on

95

i've got nothing to say

there's nothing going on

up here

nothing not even ridicule

and we've been here for

PAUL:
    nine days
    nine days
    one day left
    you're not gonna give up one day before the end

GILLES:
    i've got nothing left
    i'm
    i'm gonna die

PAUL:
    cut that crap and breathe into your bag
    and give me a break with this dying shit ok
    you're not a kid anymore
    you're a responsible adult
    with a job to do
    and you're not walking outta here
    until you've done it

GILLES:
    oh yeah
    well i'm leaving right now

        paul takes out a big revolver
        and points it at gilles

GILLES:
    don't tell me we're gonna play cowboys

PAUL:
   you're not walking outta here until

GILLES:
   you've gotta be kidding

PAUL:
   i'm not kidding
   it's loaded

      he feels like laughing
      it sounds like a sob

   you're gonna stay right here
   and you're gonna work
   hard

GILLES:
   or you're gonna shoot me
   where?
   in the forehead?
   in the heart?

      paul throws down the revolver
      gilles passes him the bag
      paul shrugs
      and breathes into the bag

   dumb bastard
   a great way to make us look
   ridiculous for eternity

PAUL:
   well i

GILLES:
   where did you get a big gun like that anyway?

      pause
      paul is the verge of hysterical laughter

97

PAUL:

at my mother's

GILLES:

it's

he starts laughing uncontrollably

PAUL:

my father's

gilles finds it half funny
half revolting

GILLES:

you want to shoot me with your father's gun?

PAUL:

yeah

GILLES:

pathetic

PAUL:

yeah

they look at each other
they try to see each other
long silence

PAUL:

is it true that
our wives are sleeping together?

GILLES:

absolutely

PAUL:

shit

GILLES:
    you really didn't know?

PAUL:
    no
    it's a bit insulting

GILLES:
    ah ha   that gets to you

PAUL:
    it's just that it never occurred to me
    i bet it bothers you

        pause

GILLES:
    you know our wives think we're having a great time
    so they're trying to have some fun too
    i don't know how i feel about it

    i don't know much of anything anymore
    i just know i'm walking out of here
    i'm leaving

        pause

PAUL:
    maybe it's better that way   why not

        pause

    but if you leave now you're not coming back

        pause

GILLES:
    it's a deal

PAUL:
    i can write you a cheque

99

GILLES:
    mail it
    whatever you want

PAUL:
    you bet

        pause

GILLES:
    what are you gonna do now?

PAUL:
    you think you're the last of the poets?
    there are others
    younger ones

GILLES:
    too true

        silence

PAUL:
    uhhh
    your bit there
    we're in the yellow pages
    maybe i'll
    i mean i just might use it
    if

GILLES:
    ah

PAUL:
    that alright with you?

GILLES:
    you can take the yellow pages the whole book
    and shove it up your ass   right up to the fontanel

        pause

100

PAUL:
the fontanel that's the hole
babies have in their heads?

GILLES:
right

pause

PAUL:
how 'bout you what are you gonna do?

GILLES:
i'm gonna go pick up my dog
aiee aiee aiee it hurts it hurts
it hurts

PAUL:
c'mon for chrissake get going   goddammit
you can drop the performance now

*gilles is one huge spasm
he grabs onto paul they fall to the floor
it's a massive heart attack
he's dying
paul gets up and looks at him
he goes to sit in his armchair*

PAUL:
i'm gonna use your slogan
it's good
lay off
you don't hafta do that

gilles dies

no really
it's a good slogan

we're in the yellow pages

they'll like it
you were right
the cool approach
reasonable
it's good
yep
it's
it's excellent

i think the customer
is gonna be pleased
ok
now a doctor
the phone
oh right

he exits

BLACKOUT